Written by:
Stephen Cosgrove
Illustrated by:
Robin James

PRICE STERN SLOAN
Los Angeles

Published by Price Stern Sloan, Inc.
Los Angeles, California

ISBN: 0-8431-2835-6

Library of Congress Catalog Number: 90-060294

10 9 8 7 6 5 4 3 2

Dedicated to Ruben Rizo and Asedro, two men who served with me well and with whom, sadly, I couldn't speak. Their spirits will always sing in my heart.

Stephen

South of south and beyond where the sun does fall lay the desert sands on the Island of Serendipity. The desert was a place of contrasts, where beauty must be looked for and, once found, never forgotten. Here purple-flowered, prickly cactuses were silhouetted in pink-shaded shards of light that had exploded in the setting sun.

Such beauty was always here if you looked in the land of Serendipity.

The creatures that lived in this desert region were also special in very different ways. There were odd little armadillos that rolled themselves into tight armored balls whenever threatened. There were long-legged rabbits that were faster than fast and could even outrun the setting sun. There were tortoises that sought the slower side of life, never having run anywhere in their lives.

Also in this land lived a swaybacked burro called Jalopy. Jalopy was content with the desert and loved the beauty all around. Often he could be seen with a purple blossom behind his great floppy ear as he stood all alone watching his friends cavort about the desert.

A special place was this southern desert, with special creatures all around.

The rabbit hopped about seeking a bit of dried grass as the armadillo and the tortoise nibbled along behind. Jalopy, like the others, munched for lunch the sparse vegetation that grew in the desert.

During the day, the little burro would stop and stick his greying muzzle into the air, and if the wind was just right, he could smell the lush green grasses that grew abundantly north of north. Although he had never been there, Jalopy had heard the stories of Tummy Bay which lay just north of the desert, but there was a mountain in the way and few had made the journey.

Day after day the desert seemed drier and less and less pretty to Jalopy, and he no longer looked for the hidden beauty of the desert. Instead, he would stop and look mournfully at the mountain to the north and close his long-lashed eyes and imagine the cool, green grasses around Tummy Bay.

"Oh," he would whisper to himself, "just to go there once to see the great wonders that must abound in all that lushness."

One day Jalopy finally decided that he would go and probably never return. Quickly, he sought his friends and said his goodbyes.

With nary a look back and with hardly a regret, he trotted off to the north. The mountain was farther than it seemed, but Jalopy was filled with the energy of new adventure. In time he found himself in the foothills, and then upon the mountain itself. It was a grand mountain and the trail was twisted and very scary indeed.

But the little burro wasn't scared, for the path of opportunity was never straight, and every step brought him closer and closer to the lushness that he knew he would find surrounding Tummy Bay.

Day turned to night and still Jalopy continued onward without any sleep, without any rest.

That poor burro had walked through the night and was nearly asleep on his feet when his ears snapped up and his eyes opened wide. He was no longer in the desert. He was knee deep in grass and clover so lush that he could taste it in the air. Kicking his hooves to the sky, he danced about the meadow braying loudly in celebration.

His celebration stopped, though, when he came to a sign posted on a pole thrust deep in the ground. The sign looked like this:

ARNINGWAY
ASTAY OUTAY
UMMYTAY ABAY!!

"That's odd," laughed Jalopy. "I can read most anything, but that gibberish makes no sense at all. It must say, 'Welcome to Tummy Bay. Eat all you can. Eat all you may!' Ha! Ha! Well thank you, sign. I do feel welcome." And with that he dropped his head down into the grass and took a great bite of purpled clover.

Jalopy ate and ate, and his belly got bigger and bigger and surely would have burst had there not come into the meadow a great gathering of pigs. They snorted and grunted as pigs were wont to do. Suddenly they threw their snouts in the air and froze in their tracks for they had seen the intruder, Jalopy.

With tiny ears flopping and corkscrew tails untwisted and straight with anger, they raced to where the burro stood nervously, obviously in the middle of *their* meadow by the bay. "Uh, hello," said Jalopy. "You guys sure have a great meadow here. I just love it. I have some friends back home and I tell you what, they would love it, too!"

The pigs looked at him as he babbled on, and then a great boar stomped up to Jalopy and bellowed, "Atwhay aray ouya oingday erehay? Antcay ouyay eadray ethay ignsay?"

Jalopy shook his head until his ears snapped, and listened and listened again. No matter how hard he listened, he couldn't understand a word that was spoken.

The great pig repeated his challenge over and over, but no matter how many times he heard it, Jalopy couldn't make any sense from the gutteral utterings. The little burro was quite nervous for he meant no harm. "Gee whiz, pigs," he stammered. "I don't know what you're saying, but gosh this sure is a neat place you have here. I just love it."

The great boar just snorted in disgust, "Ouya aray upidstay ikelay allay ethay othersay atthay omecay romfay ethay outhsay." To the other pigs he shouted, "Ovemay imhay otay ethay edgeay ofay ethay eadowmay anday ontday etlay imhay ovemay. Atwhay aay ummyday!"

Jalopy still couldn't figure out what he had said, but it was easy to tell that they wanted him to move. The pigs rudely bumped and pushed him in the direction they wanted him to go.

The pigs shoved that poor little burro to the very edge of the meadow. There they watched him suspiciously with their tiny piggy eyes. Every time he would bend his head to take a bite of grass, one of the pigs would rush at him and shout, “Opstay! Opstay! Ummyday!!”

It didn’t take Jalopy long to figure out that they wanted him to stop trying to eat, so he stopped. He waited and waited as the older and larger pigs mumbled and grumbled at the other end of Tummy Bay. While he waited, the little piglets came, the children. Now Jalopy had always loved children no matter the make or model, and these children were no exception.

He laughed as they ran about his legs, chanting nonsense that he couldn’t understand.

“Ummyday! Ummyday! Urrobay, ummyday. Eshay osay atfay, eshay otgay aay igbay ummytay! Ummyday, ummyday, atwhay aay ummyday!”

Finally, one small pig with a bow in her hair ran the children off and waddled up to Jalopy. With sad brown eyes she looked at the little burro, and he looked back at her. There was so much warmth in Jalopy's eyes that it melted the little pig's heart, and she resolved to teach Jalopy how to speak their language.

Carefully she reached down and pulled a long blade of grass from the ground. "Rassgay," she grunted as she shook the grass.

Jalopy bent down, and with half-moon eyes watching, he too pulled a blade of grass from the ground. "Hmmm," he thought. "She's trying to teach me. Rassgay must mean grass. That's it!" And with that he shouted out loud, "Rassgay! Rassgay!" as the pig nodded with satisfaction.

Word by word, Jalopy learned to speak the language of Tummy Bay. Like a child learning words for the very first time, he stumbled at first and then carefully began to pronounce the awkward words that made up the pigs' language. Because he was with one of the pigs, Jalopy was allowed free run of Tummy Bay, although the other pigs didn't really trust him. As he walked by, they would grunt, "Ummyday, ummyday," and then just laugh and laugh.

In time, Jalopy learned to speak the language well, and when he was fluent all the pigs gathered around. When they spoke, Jalopy listened and knew exactly what they said.

"Welcome to Tummy Bay," grunted the boar proudly. "Now that you speak the language so well, we would be proud to have you stay and live your life in our meadow."

"Ankthay ouya," said Jalopy just like a native. He looked about and then shocked them one and all when he said, "But I don't want to stay."

"Ummyday," grunted one of the pigs to another.

"Onay," said Jalopy. "Iay amay onay ummyday, I am no dummy. For when I was a stranger and didn't understand, you laughed at me and called me names, hiding behind your language. Now that you can't hide, you really have nothing to say that I want to hear."

With the embarrassed pigs watching, Jalopy packed some lush, long grasses on his back and began the long journey back to the deserts south of south. There he would teach the others how to speak pig latin, for if they ever traveled north, they would need this shield of language for protection.

Yes, Jalopy went home, not because he was hurt by silly names hurled in ignorance, but rather for the love of his true friends. For the grass always seems greener on the other side of the mountain.

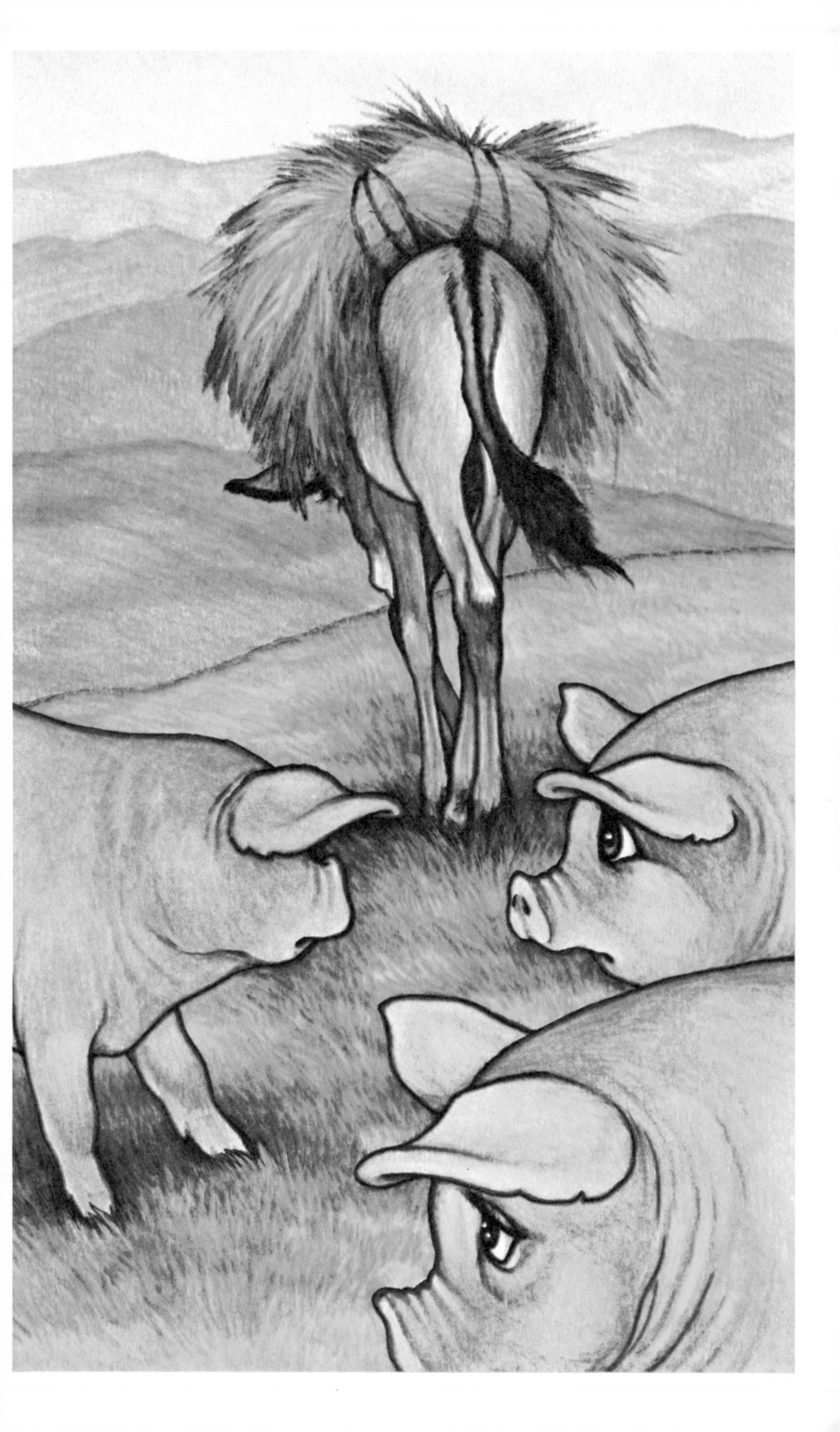

IF YOU HIDE BEHIND YOUR LANGUAGE
ONLY WORDS THAT YOU CAN SAY
REMEMBER A BURRO CALLED JALOPY
AND HIS DAY AT UMMYTAY BAY

Written by Stephen Cosgrove
Illustrated by Robin James

Enjoy all the delightful books in the Serendipity Series:

BANGALEE	LEO THE LOP TAIL THREE
BUTTERMILK	LITTLE MOUSE ON THE PRAIRIE
BUTTERMILK BEAR	MAUI-MAUI
CATUNDRA	MEMILY
CRABBY GABBY	MING LING
CREOLE	MINIKIN
CRICKLE-CRACK	MISTY MORGAN
DRAGOLIN	MORGAN AND ME
THE DREAM TREE	MORGAN AND YEW
FANNY	MORGAN MINE
FEATHER FIN	MORGAN MORNING
FLUTTERBY	THE MUFFIN MUNCHER
FLUTTERBY FLY	MUMKIN
FRAZZLE	NITTER PITTER
GABBY	PERSNICKITY
GLITTERBY BABY	PISH POSH
THE GNOME FROM NOME	POPPYSEED
GRAMPA-LOP	RAZ-MA-TAZ
THE GRUMPLING	RHUBARB
HUCKLEBUG	SASSAFRAS
JALOPY	SERENDIPITY
JINGLE BEAR	SNIFFLES
KARTUSCH	SQUABBLES
KIYOMI	SQUEAKERS
LADY ROSE	TICKLE'S TALE
LEO THE LOP	TRAPPER
LEO THE LOP TAIL TWO	WHEEDLE ON THE NEEDLE

ZIPPITY ZOOM

The above books, and many others, can be bought wherever books are sold, or may be ordered directly from the publisher.

PRICE STERN SLOAN
Los Angeles